D0510720

THE STICK MAN WITH A BIG BUM

Eric (the Stick Man) Trum

Jonny Staples

Copyright 2014
First Print Edition Published June 2014
All rights reserved
This book is sold subject to the condition
that is shall not, by way of trade or otherwise
be lent, hired out or otherwise circulated
in any form of binding or cover other than that
In which it is published.

'Why fit in when you were born to stand out?'

-Dr Seuss

Introduction from Eric (the stick man) Trum

Well hello there, I'm Eric Trum, and this is a picture of me.

Yes, yes, I know….. I have a rather large bum. For some reason people keep telling me about my bottom, as if they think I haven't noticed or something.

Well I have noticed. I notice every time I sit down,

and end up being higher up than I expected.

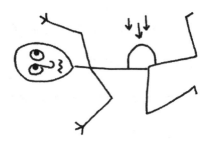

And I notice every time I fall over and find myself

on the floor, pinned down by my own behind.

This bottom of mine really does cause a lot of problems. The worst thing is that sometimes people make rude comments about it.

'Hey big bum', someone yelled yesterday.

'Wow, I bet you struggle on a bicycle', someone else said last week. Terrible, some people are sooooooo rude.

Apparently it is rather unusual for stick men to have big bottoms, in fact, stick men are kind of famous for not having bums at all. This makes the whole thing all the more embarrassing.... So PLEASE don't look at my bottom in ANY of the pictures in this book from now on. Agreed? Good!

Just look at my extremely sensible face, or my rather nice hands instead.

Thank you.

Great, I'm glad that has all been sorted out, and remember, nobody's perfect. I think life would be very dull if all stick men looked the same, so I have saved you from a life of tedious stick man sameness. Hooray for me.

Right, let me tell you a bit more about this book.

Well, it all began when Jonny did a doodle of a stick man while he was on the phone to his friend Firna. He wasn't really concentrating on the picture and doodled a large bottom onto the character. Now, I don't know why he did it, and he says he doesn't know why he did it, but it happened. The bum was added and now we all have to live with it.

After the phone call Jonny walked away, leaving his doodle book open on the table. I was just lying there, on the paper, where I'd been drawn. After a few minutes, I started to feel really strange, like I was coming alive. I suddenly found that I could move my legs, then, a minute later, I managed to move all of my body and sat up. I was amazed to discover that I wasn't attached to the paper anymore. I was free! It was a very weird feeling and I just stared ahead in shock for a while.

'Hello,' I called out eventually. Jonny rushed back into the room and knelt down next to me, looking at me for a long time. His mouth was open and his head slowly shook from side to side. His face looked massive and, at that moment, I realised that I must be pretty small.

'Hello,' he said, looking at me very carefully.

'Hi,' I said.

'This is so weird. Are you the stick man I just drew?'

I nodded.

'Amazing,' Jonny said, 'none of my drawings have ever come alive before. Wow, you're like a real little person.'

I tried to stand up but I couldn't, so I just rocked about on my bottom looking at him.

'So' said Jonny, 'what are we going to do with you?'

I wanted to raise my shoulders in an 'I don't know' kind of a way, but I found that I didn't really have shoulders, so I just raised my arms.

Jonny smiled at me, 'well you can live in a shoe box in my room,' he said.

'Ummmm, I don't want to stay in a shoe box,' I said, 'I want to do lots of fun things.' I was surprised to find that I spoke in an incredibly high voice and I could see Jonny wincing.

'Blimey,' he said, 'I didn't expect you to sound like

that.'

'Well I have just been drawn,' I said, 'so I'm sort of a baby, and I think babies have quite high voices.'

'Yes, I suppose so,' said Jonny.

'So what can I do to keep busy?' I asked, looking around the room for ideas. 'I'm sure I don't want to sit around all day with nothing to do.'

'Well,' said Jonny, tapping my feet with a pencil,

'It sounds like we need to find you some activities.'

I gently kicked at the pencil while Jonny smiled. 'Right,' he said, 'I've got it! Let's think of loads of fun things to do, and then we'll write a book about those things. Then, if anyone else is ever bored, or doesn't know what to do, they can try them too.'

My eyes opened very wide with excitement. I

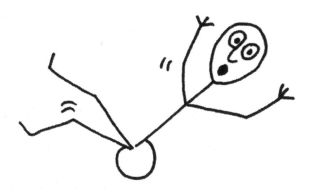

jumped up and then fell down straight away, as my bum was so heavy it kind of pulled me over.

'Why did you give me such a big bum?' I said, as I lay on the floor.

'Sorry, I don't know really, I guess I thought it would look funny,' said Jonny as he tried to help me up with his pencil, 'I didn't actually expect you to come alive you know.'

'Well, can you rub it out?' I asked.

Jonny looked at his pencil and we both noticed that the rubber had been chewed off, 'sorry,' he said, 'anyway, I don't think you'll be able to rub bits out now that you're alive, besides, it gives you character.'

After a lot of ridiculous struggling, with me hanging onto the pencil for dear life, I managed to get up again and we started researching ideas for the book.

It was then that I had my moment of genius. I was so excited I couldn't speak for a while and just stood there with one of my eyes throbbing fiercely.

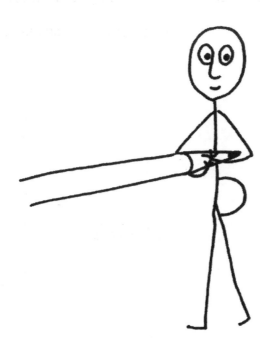

'What is it?' asked Jonny.

'Well,' I said, 'why don't I try out every activity we think of, and then I can write a bit about how each one went for me. That way it will be a very interesting book for both humans and stick men.'

I watched Jonny's face, hoping he'd agree.

'Good idea Eric,' he said and we shook hands.

'Um, why am I called Eric?' I asked.

'I don't know,' he replied, 'it just kind of suits

you. Yes, I'm going to call you Eric Trum.'

I sat on Jonny's shoulder and we got to work. We found loads of brilliant activities to try and the rest of the book describes how we got on with them. Read on if you want to find out why we laughed, discover why we thumped the ground in fury, and see just how many times my bum got stuck in things….. oh the joy, (hmmmmmmmm.)

ACTIVITY NUMBER 1

Make Copper Coins Super Shiny

'OK,' said Jonny, 'the first activity we are going to do, is to bling our copper.

'What?' I asked, looking at him as if he had gone completely mad.

'Well, I've found a way to make dull brown copper coins shiny and amazing,' he said. He then explained the whole thing to me, and I must say I was very interested.

METHOD

For this activity all you need are old copper coins, a bowl and some lemon juice.

Put the coins in the bowl and cover them with the lemon juice (no overlapping), Leave them for ten minutes, then pull them out, rinse and....

TA DA!!!

Amazing shiny coins

Whaaaaa hoooooooo

I only had one coin (booo hooo), which I'd found under the fridge next to an old grape, so I used that for this activity.

As I didn't have enough coins to justify using a bowl, I used a little eggcup with a painting of a chick on it. I dropped my lucky penny in, added the juice and waited. It actually worked very well and I was pleased with my shiny coin. I could almost see my reflection in it and it was just the right size for me to balance on. (Remember; don't look at my bottom in the following picture.)

(I saw you looking! Please don't look again.)

BONUS FACT!!!

My penny is so beautiful that I can't bear to spend it now so I have decided to save it in a money jar. I am going to save up for a small rubber duck, as I think that would make bath time much better.

(Total money in the rubber duck fund so far – one penny.)

I placed the penny in the jar and it fell into place with a satisfying clink.

Jonny let me borrow one of his coins so I could have another go at the activity. This time I carefully put small dots of juice on the surface using a cotton bud. Later on, after rinsing the juice off, I ended up with a very nice polka dot coin....

'Cool Bananas'... (Did I really just say that?)

Unfortunately I wasn't allowed to keep that coin as Jonny wanted to buy a very small cola bottle sweet with it. He gave me the last quarter of his sweet though, but as soon as I'd put it in my mouth I went all funny, as it was extremely sour. My eyes still haven't gone back to normal and my legs went wobbly. In fact, my legs went so wobbly that I fell backwards into the eggcup with the lemon juice in it! I was stuck for over an hour.

WARNING – never sit in a bowl of lemon juice, it kind of stings.

Apart from the falling into an eggcup bit, this activity was quite fun, and it is very nice to have an extremely shiny coin. I would recommend this to both humans and stick men.

SCIENCE BIT

When the copper from the coin mixes with the oxygen in the air an oxide builds up, which makes the surface of the coin turn brown.

Lemon juice reacts with the oxide and removes it from the coin, leaving it super shiny.

Jonny wrote that last bit. I did tell him off about it, but he said that people want to know about that kind of thing.

He may try to add other bits to the book now and then but I'll try and warn you if I see one coming up.

So... moving swiftly on, what's next???????

ACTIVITY NUMBER 2

Write in a Secret Code

When I found out we were doing this I was actually quite excited because I quite like the idea of secrets

and secret messages. We researched different codes
and decided to try out this simple one.

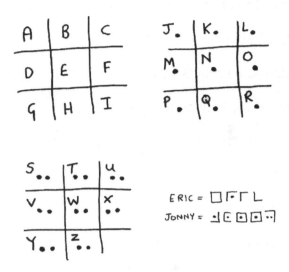

ERIC = □ ⌐ ⌐ L

JONNY = ⌐| ⊏ ⊡ ⊡ ⫽

Jonny gave me a piece of paper with these strange
grids drawn on it. 'This is the key to the code,' he
said.

'I don't get it' I said, scratching my head.

'Well,' said Jonny, each letter is a drawing of a bit
of the grid. Look, I'll give you some more examples.'

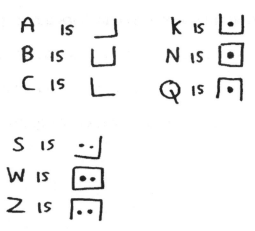

A is ⅃   K is ⊡(with dot right)
B is ⊔   N is ⊡(with dot)
C is L   Q is ⌐⦁

S is ∙∙⅃
W is ⊡(two dots)
Z is ⌐∙∙⌐

'Ah ha,' I said after studying his examples for one hour, 'I get it now.'

We wrote each other a few messages and then tried to read them. Later on in the day I thought of a brilliant way to make this activity even more fun. I wrote a note for Jonny, and then went to the local charity shop where I hid it in the back of a book called '100 Things to do with a Parsnip,'

It was very difficult climbing up to the bookshelf and I did get stuck between two old beano annuals for a while. Anyway, in the end, I managed to get the message into the book and climb back down again.

Just as I'd left the shop I realised that I'd left the bit of paper with the key on it in the book too. Doh! Oh well, I thought, I'll get it back once Jonny buys the book.

'I suggest you buy '100 Things to do with a Parsnip,' from the Purple Cross charity shop if you want to read my message,' I said casually as we had lunch.

'Oh Eric Trum, what am I going to do with you?' he said as he put me in his pocket and raced down to the shop.

'Have you got 100 Things to do with a Parsnip?' he asked the shopkeeper.

'Sorry,' he said, shaking his head, 'that person just bought it.' He pointed to a rather large man with a long moustache, who was leaving the shop.

'That's my neighbour, Jeremy Mothballs,' whispered Jonny as we watched the man walk out.

OH NO!! All that work and Jonny wouldn't be able to read my message! I'd spent an hour on it as well so I was rather angry. The message was a poem about having a big bottom.

⊡⊡϶⊡⌐/϶⊔⊔⊡/⊏Ŀ⊡/ϵ⊏/⅃/⅂⊔⌐∟⊔/϶⅃⊡

Hang on; it's going to take you ages to translate all that, so I'll write it in English.

Never make fun of a stick man

Who happens to have a big bum

Because normal is boring

Normal is dull

Let's all be different

And life will be brill

Then I remembered that the piece of paper with the key to the code on it was left in the book too. So

Jeremy Mothballs will definitely be able to decipher it, which means it's not a secret message at all. I stamped on my own toe as a punishment.

I was also rather angry because I had been looking forward to reading '100 Things to do with a Parsnip.' I'd had a sneaky look at it while I was in the charity shop and was particularly interested in thing number 37 - 'make a giraffe out of a parsnip'.

Apart from the missing message upset, this was an extremely good activity and there are lots of other codes available online (or you could make up your own). I had a go at making one up. Can you guess what it says?

(Answer: stickman + big bum = stickman with a big bum) (p.s. don't look at the bum)

ACTIVITY NUMBER 3

String Telephone

'I've got a new activity planned,' said Jonny one week later. When he showed me this idea I was pleased because I thought I'd be small enough to use the string as some sort of zip wire slide, as well as using it as a telephone.

METHOD

Here is a picture how to do it. You get two yogurt pots and make a small hole in the bottom of each one. You then thread one end of a looooooooooong piece of string through one hole and tie a knot, and then do the same with the other end of the string.

After that you make sure the string is tight with no bends in it. One person stands at each end of the string and you chat away into the pots.

How it went for us

We ate some strawberry yogurts (YUM) then cleaned out the pots to use.

I stood on the bedroom windowsill next to the plastic pot, and Jonny stood in the mud at the bottom of the garden with the other pot. We then had a go at communicating.

'Fool,' I shouted into the yogurt pot while waving my arms around. I wouldn't normally call Jonny a fool, but I didn't think the string telephone would actually work, so I was rather shocked to see him shaking his fist at me.

'I'll scribble you out if you're rude like that,' he replied. It was so weird because I could hear him really loudly even though he was far away and looked really small.

I then tied the yogurt pot onto the window frame, sat on the string and, weeeeeeeeeeeeeeee, slid right down into the garden.

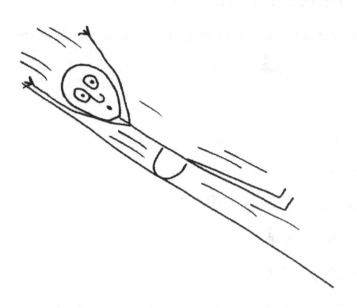

'I was only joking,' I said, rubbing my burnt, sore bottom and hopping about in the mud.

'OK, back upstairs now so we can test the telephone more', he said ushering me away. I ran back up and jumped back onto the windowsill, leaving tiny muddy footprints behind me.

'Question time,' he said into the cup.

I jumped up and down because I love answering questions. I waited eagerly next to the pot.

'I'm ready,' I said very, very quietly. I was mega surprised because he actually heard me, even though I'd spoken in a very quiet whisper.

'OK,' he said, 'What's the longest word in the English language?'

Hmmm, I stood on my head (difficult) and I balanced on my bottom (easy), as I tried to think of an answer.

'Supercalywhatstheword?' I said into the yogurt pot. 'No,' said Jonny, 'It's 'smiles' because there is a mile in between the first and last letter.' I could hear him laughing and, when I looked out of the window, he was slapping his thigh with a look of delight on his face.

'Very good,' I said, 'OK, I've got one, 'what has to be broken before you can use it?' I smiled smugly, as I knew he wouldn't get it.

'An egg?' he said.

'Yes,' I replied.

Well, overall it was a great day and I will definitely be using the yogurt pot telephone on a regular basis from now on.

SCIENCE BIT

When the first person talks into their pot, the bottom vibrates with the sound waves of their voice. The vibrations travel through the string causing that to vibrate too. This makes the second cup vibrate, producing the same sound waves which travel into the ear to be translated by the brain.

Yes, thank you for that Jonny.

NUMBER 4

Penny Throwing Competition

It was on the day of the penny throwing activity that I first met Jonny's neighbour, Jeremy Mothballs. I'll tell you about him later. First let me tell you how to do this excellent activity.

METHOD

All you need are some coins, a wall and a dressing gown cord or belt. It was good weather so we decided to try doing this game in the garden. I ran about with Jonny's purple dressing gown cord trailing behind me, and tipped my one shiny penny out of my rubber duck savings jar. I leapt down the stairs and went out into the garden.

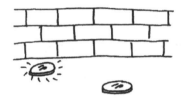

The idea behind this game is that everyone stands behind a line (made by the dressing gown cord), and then throws their coin against a wall. Whoever throws the coin that lands closest to the wall is the winner.

Jonny said that some people play it so that the winner takes all the coins and keeps them but, as I only had one coin, we would play for points instead.

We were having so much fun with this game that, at first, we didn't notice someone watching us over the wall.

'What are you doing?' A man said, peering down at us. I recognised him as Jonny's neighbour, the man we'd seen in the charity shop.

We jumped with surprise as we looked up at him.

'Oh, um, just playing a game,' said Jonny.

'I'm coming round, I've got loads of pennies,' said Jeremy Mothballs.

Jonny and I exchanged a worried glance and I chewed on the end of my hand as we waited.

A few minutes later he was in the garden with us.

'So who's this?' he asked, pointing at me.

'Oh, um this is Eric Trum,' said Jonny.

The man smirked, 'Eric Trum with a big bum,' he sang. We went quiet.

'Um Eric, this is my neighbour, Jeremy Mothballs,' said Jonny.

Jeremy placed his muddy boot ON Jonny's dressing gown cord and threw a coin against the wall. Jonny and I then threw our coins. We covered our eyes with our hands, as we saw that Jeremy's coin was by far the closest. Jonny got his pen out to give him a point when Jeremy grabbed all three coins.'

'I'm done now', he said, leaving the garden.

I stared as I watched him walk away with my very shiny penny. My rubber duck penny!!! My fund was now EMPTY!!!!. I felt hollow inside. Jonny gave me one of his spare pennies and we carried on with the game, but from that day on I knew I had to get Jeremy Mothballs back.

ACTIVITY NUMBER 5

Mysterious Crystal Ball Making

Well, one week later we were warming our feet by the fire when it started to snow! Huge snowflakes tumbled down and I was very excited, as I had never seen snow before. I jumped up onto the windowsill and placed my hands against the cold glass.

'Can I go out there?' I asked.

'Of course,' said Jonny. He then wrapped me in a sweet wrapper and I rushed out to try and catch the flakes.

Later that day Jonny said he had the perfect idea for activity number 5. 'Let's make crystal balls,' he said.

This involved getting some small balloons and filling them with water. We filled six balloons all together and I enjoyed bouncing on them for a while.

Once I'd finished tumbling around we carefully took the balloons outside and placed them in the snow on the small lawn in front of our house.

'As long as it's cold enough the water inside the balloons should freeze,' said Jonny, 'leaving us with ice balls.'

I was so excited as I stood next to the balloons, waiting.

'It won't happen straight away,' said Jonny, 'it could take a few days, and the temperature has to be below 0 degrees before it even starts to work.

SCIENCE BIT

The freezing point of water is the temperature at which water changes from a liquid into a solid. This is usually at 0 degrees centigrade.

Well, I didn't sleep well that night. I kept wondering if the water was freezing yet. I got up in the night to have a look and had to slip through the letterbox. I ended up tiptoeing across the snowy lawn in the dark. My feet were absolutely freezing and it got the point where my toes were completely numb. I touched one of the balloons and it did feel hard, but when I pushed it, a thin layer of ice behind the rubber cracked so I went back to bed.

The next morning I raced out, waded through the snow to the balloons and HOORAY, they were quite solid. Jonny cut the rubber and removed it, and we were left with six Ice balls. They weren't solid right through though. Only the outside of the balls had frozen and the water from the inside dripped away leaving lovely hollow spheres.

I managed to get inside one of the balls and stood looking out at the world. It was amazing but rather cold. Jonny had these little battery-powered candles left over from Christmas, and he put one in each of the other balls. They looked really good. We went inside and looked at our brilliant creations through the window. We then saw Jeremy Mothballs leaving his house. He was carrying a rather shiny penny. Hmmmmm!

'How are we going to get Jeremy back for taking our money?' I asked Jonny.

'I'm not sure Eric,' Jonny replied, 'let's see if activity Number 6 can help.'

ACTIVITY NUMBER 6

The Coin Prank

One week later the snow had melted and there was a little bit of winter sun shining through the clouds. I was in the front garden, putting my head in a snowdrop flower when Jonny came out. 'I've got the perfect prank to play on Jeremy Mothballs,' he said, waving a penny around. He had a big grin on his face.

'Go on?' I said, falling over forwards and getting my head stuck in the flower. After a bit of a kerfuffle

I managed to get my head out and stood, eagerly waiting.

Jonny told me about the coin prank and I agreed that it was an excellent idea.

METHOD

For this activity, Jonny used his penny and a tube of superglue. We super glued the coin onto the pavement near our house and then went inside and sat at the window, watching and waiting for Jeremy to come along.

During the day, three other people walked by and, when they noticed the coin, each one of them tried to pick it up. When they found out it was stuck to the ground, they shook their head and walked on. Watching them was slightly funny, but we were really waiting for Jeremy, (now known as Jeremy the Enemy.)

Eventually Jeremy Mothballs came along, his head swinging and his shoulders back. He noticed the coin straight away and tried to pick it up. When he couldn't, he shouted angrily, and then he sat down on the pavement, picking at the coin. It was no use, the coin didn't move at all. 'Idiot coin,' he shouted before storming into his house and slamming the door. Jonny and I watched, hidden behind the curtain.

A few minutes later he came out again, this time he was armed with a knife, which he used to try and prise the coin up. We were giggling and whispering to each other about how funny it was when Jeremy suddenly flew backwards as the coin came loose. The penny flew into the air and Jeremy ran to get it, picked it up and took it into his house.

Jonny and I stared at each other in disbelief. Jeremy now had three of our coins.

'Drat,' I said, before rolling onto my tummy and thumping the ground.

'We'll find a way to get our money back,' said Jonny, as he lay beside me. He started thumping the ground too.

ACTIVITY NUMBER 7

Sweet Sorting

We decided we needed to do something mega fun to take our mind of Jeremy, so Jonny suggested having a sweet sorting competition.

He got a jar of jellybeans out of his corduroy bag and placed it neatly on the kitchen table next to the green tea pot. (Note - you can probably use other squidgy sweets if you don't like jellybeans.)

He then put all the jellybeans into a bowl surrounded by empty saucers. 'The idea is to pick up a sweet by sucking though the straw and then, holding the suck, move it into one of the saucers,' he said, 'you have to keep doing this until all the colours are in separate groups.'

Note - You don't have to use saucers; you could use eggcups or bowls. (I didn't want to risk using eggcups though)

Jonny went first and sorted the sweets into separate piles in two minutes; he was very pleased with himself and even ate an orange one to celebrate.

After his celebration, Jonny came up to me with a straw in his mouth. 'Your head is a bit like a jelly bean,' he said. He began chasing me around the house and I ended up hiding under the bookshelf for a while.

Eventually I came out and it was my turn to have a go at sorting the sweets.

Jonny mixed all the colours up again and I looked into the bright sea of jellybeans. I took a deep breath and then started trying to move one bean. It was hard for me to even fit the straw in my mouth, let alone suck, and it took me thirteen hours and sixteen minutes to sort them out.

Now, I'm not sure that this game was fair because each jellybean was the size of one quarter of my head. Now imagine if you were trying to pick up something the size of one quarter of your head.... with a straw!!!!!

It was extremely difficult and I felt quite strange for several hours afterwards.

INTERESTING FACT

At the time of writing, the world record for sorting 30 jellybeans appears to be 16.88 seconds. Quite fast.

<u>Suitability Roundup</u>

Suitability for humans: 8 out of 10

Suitability for stick men: 0 out of 10

ACTIVITY NUMBER 8

Squirt Toy

It took me three weeks to recover from the jellybean-sorting incident. I'd been lying in bed for most of that time, trying not to dream about giant jellybeans.

Anyway, on a nice warm morning in February Jonny called me downstairs. 'We need to get cracking on with the activities,' he said.

'OK, I think I'm ready,' I said from under my blanket.

'Good, because I've got a really good idea,' he shouted.

I rolled out of bed and bounced down the stairs on my bum. I found Jonny in the kitchen holding two empty plastic water bottles.

'Good morning,' I said, helping myself to a cheerio, 'what are we doing then?'

'We're going to use these bottles to make squirt toys,' he said, his eyes shining.

'Sounds quite good,' I said, filling a thimble with apple juice.

He then made a small hole in the lid of each bottle, filled the bottles with water, put the lids on and started squirting me with the cold liquid.

'What are you doing,' I shrieked, leaping around trying to avoid the spray.

'It's a squirt toy, here' he said handing one to me.

'OK, but let's do it in the garden,' I said, carrying

mine outside.

Once outside I managed to get Jonny back and

gave him a right good soaking. Then I had a brilliant

idea. I balanced some corks along the garden wall and we took it in turns to try and squirt them off. After one particularly good squirt I heard a growl coming from the other side of the wall. I then saw Jeremy Mothballs, dripping wet, staring at us.

'What are you doing?' he growled.

'Oh sorry, just a game,' Jonny said.

'Where's my penny?' I said.

'I won it fare and square,' said Jeremy before going off. I heard him filling a bucket from his garden tap so we rushed inside to hide.

Overall I think the squirt toy game is pretty good, as long as who ever you squirt agrees to be squirted. If no one agrees, then line up some lightweight items such as empty drink cans or corks and squirt them instead.

CONFESSION

I am secretly glad I squirted Jeremy Mothballs.

Ratings

Danger rating: 8 out of 10

Fun rating: 9 out of 10

ACTIVITY NUMBER 9

Pipe Cleaner People

Jonny ran into the house the next afternoon carrying a mysterious bag with the words 'craft shop', on it.

'What is it? What is it?' I said, jumping up and trying to grab onto the side of the bag.

'Calm down, little guy,' he said, lowering himself onto the sofa. 'It's just the items needed for activity number nine.' From the look on his face I could tell that activity number nine was going to be something very good.

He slowly reached into the bag and pulled out a packet of multi coloured pipe cleaners.

I looked at their bright fluffiness with great interest, they looked pleasingly soft and I longed to feel them. He got one out and handed it to me. I bent it in half and was surprised to see that it kept its shape.

'What are we going to do with them?' I asked.

He then explained how to make amazing pipe cleaner people.

METHOD

Take two pipe cleaners. Fold pipe cleaner one in half and make a loop for the head in the middle. Twist the two strands together for the body and leave two bits loose for the legs. Then take the second pipe cleaner and twist the middle of it around the body lots of times, leaving two arms sticking out.

Once we'd made one I stared at it in amazement. It looked quite a lot like me (but without the bottom of course.) We made four pipe cleaner people altogether and they all looked brilliant.

I danced around the room with the yellow one and pretended it was alive (don't tell anyone).

'That's not the end of it though,' said Jonny, taking the red pipe cleaner person by the hand, 'we now have to find funny places to put them.'

We looked all around the house and hung one from the bottom of a lampshade, had one hanging out of the letterbox and had another clinging onto the light switch cord in the bathroom. 'Let's put the green one outside somewhere,' said Jonny, 'to make the garden look even better.'

I nodded eagerly and we raced outside. In the end we sat him on the fence looking into Jeremy's garden. We giggled as we ran back inside and got ourselves drinks to celebrate. A cup of tea for Jonny and a very small glass of peach juice for me, perfect.

AND NOW FOR THE BAD NEWS

It was a lovely activity and we very pleased with ourselves for making such fantastic pipe cleaner people and then Jeremy the Enemy had to go and spoil it. I will explain what happened, but, if you are someone who gets angry or upset easily, you may want to skip this bit and move onto the next activity.

Well, the very next day we went out into the garden to check on the little pipe cleaner person we'd left on the fence. We saw him straight away but he looked very different. His pipe cleaner body was the same, but tied onto it, in the place where a bottom might be, was a huge green balloon. We ran over for a closer look and saw that there was writing on the balloon; it said 'Big Bum Trum,' in enormous black letters. We stared, speechless for a while.

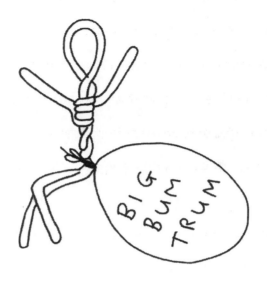

'Why did you have to call me Eric Trum,' I said to Jonny, 'why did you have to give me a name that rhymes with bum?' I ran into the house crying.

I felt bad for shouting at Jonny; after all, Jeremy Mothballs was the mean one.

ACTIVITY NUMBER 10

Conundrum Solving

The next day Jonny sat next to me on the sofa and put his arm around my little non-shoulder area. 'Are you ready to do thing number 10?' he said. I nodded while looking straight ahead.

He then got out a notebook, 'I've got ten conundrums for you, because thing number ten is conundrum solving.' I cheered up after that because solving puzzles is quite fun. I got into my conundrum solving position and waited.

THE CONUNDRUMS

Here are the ten conundrums that Jonny gave me. See if you can solve them, then check the answers. We can compare how well we did at the end of this section.

One - *Ben's mother had 4 children. The first one was called May. The second was called June and* the third was called July. What was the fourth child's name?

Two - A man says that he can predict the score of any football match before it even begins. He is right. How is this possible?

Three - What is full of holes but still holds water?

Four - How can you place a pencil on the floor so that no one can jump over it?

Five - What has a thumb and four fingers but is not a hand?

Six - What is orange and sounds like a parrot?

Seven - What goes from side to side and up and down but never moves?

Eight - What is as big as an elephant but weighs nothing?

Nine - How could all of your cousins have an aunt who is not your aunt?

Ten - You are in a race and you overtake the

person in second place. What place are you now in?

I spent quite a long time on these. In fact I stayed up late into the night chewing on the end of my pencil while trying to work them out. In the end I managed to get one right.... Number 8.

Read on to find the answers.

How many did you get correct?

Answers

One - *Ben*

Two - *He says that the score <u>before</u> the game begins is 0:0, which is correct.*

Three - *A sponge*

Four - *Place it next to the wall*

Five - *A glove*

Six - *A carrot*

Seven - *A road*

Eight - *An elephant's shadow*

Nine - *Your mum is their aunt*

Ten - *Second place*

CONCLUSION

If you got more than two right, then you are some sort of genius.

If you got one right then you are quite clever (like me).

If you got none right, then... never mind.

If you got loads right then wow ze dowsee (did I just say that? I think I did, oh dear).

 Overall it was a fun day and, because I was so busy trying to figure the answers out, I forgot all about Jeremy Mothballs and the balloon bum.

ACTIVITY NUMBER 11

Blindfolded Breakfast

'Quick Eric, come downstairs, I've got a surprise for you,' Jonny shouted the next morning. I stretched my little stick arms and yawned before rolling out of bed and making my way into the bright yellow kitchen.

'What's the surprise?' I asked, as I opened the cupboard and got out a piece of bread.

'Well, you won't be needing that for a start,' said Jonny, taking the bread off me and putting it away, 'because today you are having a blindfolded breakfast.'

'I'm blindfolding my bread?' I asked.

'No, your bread won't be blindfolded, you will.'

I looked him and bit my fingers; I wasn't too sure about being blindfolded. Jonny was busy getting a small piece of material out of his pocket while I sat quietly wondering what was going to happen.

'Don't worry, it'll be all nice things,' said Jonny.

METHOD

This activity involves one person being blindfolded while the other person feeds them different foods. The blindfolded person has to try and guess what has been placed on their tongue.

So, there I sat with a small blindfold covering my eyes as I waited, wondering what my first treat would be...

YUMALICIOUS, it was soft and squashy. 'It's a miniature marshmallow,' I shrieked. I smiled and started to enjoy the activity.

'Very good,' Jonny said, before placing another item on my tongue.

'AGHHHHHHHAAA YUK,' I shouted, spitting it out and wiping my mouth on my arm. 'What was that?'

'It was a bit of pickled onion,' laughed Jonny.

'But you said everything would be nice,' I said.

'Pickled onions are nice,' he replied, before feeding me the third thing.

We continued the game for quite a while. Here is a list of all the things I tasted...

A marshmallow

A pickled onion

Cheese

A cheerio

Jelly

Bread

A chocolate covered ant

Liquorish

A peppermint sweet

Mustard

I guessed most of them right.

I think the worst one for me was the mustard. I was expecting something sweet so my tongue went into shock as soon as it was applied.

I have to say it was the most unusual breakfast I have ever had. I did find out that cereal and jelly taste good together though, so this activity has given me a new menu option.

After my go, we swapped round and I blindfolded Jonny with his green scarf. I couldn't think of many new ideas, so I gave him seven chocolates, which he was rather pleased about.

ACTIVITY NUMBER 12

Peppermint Sweet Making

Digging out the peppermint sweets during the blindfolded breakfast the day before had reminded Jonny about peppermint sweet making. He decided that it would be a good activity for us to try.

METHOD

Get the following ingredients

1 cup of icing sugar

4 teaspoons of milk

A few drops of green food colouring (optional)

One quarter of a teaspoon of peppermint essence

Extra bit of icing sugar (for dusting).

'Right, we've got everything ready,' said Jonny, eating a teaspoon full of icing sugar.

I stood on an upside down cup, and looked into the brown mixing bowl, waiting for the magic to happen. Just as I was balancing, my heavy bum made me fall over backwards... straight into the bag of icing sugar! A huge cloud of white dust flew into the air as I scrabbled about in the white powder. Jonny pulled me out with a spoon and deposited me on the worktop. I kept falling backwards leaving white round bum prints all over the place. In the end I managed to

stand up and was trying to lick my face as Jonny

brushed me with a tea towel. The icing sugar didn't

brush off that well though and I was very white for

the rest of the day.

Jonny opened the window and we started cooking.

We mixed the icing sugar, milk, food colouring and

peppermint essence together until it formed a putty

like dough. Next, we dusted the worktop with icing sugar before making the dough into lots of little balls.

It was so much fun making the balls, and I must admit to eating some of the mixture when no one was looking.

I jumped on each ball, to make it a bit flatter, and then we placed them all on a piece of wax paper.

'What do we do now?' I asked.

'We need to wait for them to dry, then turn them over and dry the other side,' said Jonny, reading from the instructions.

I wasn't too keen on waiting; I wanted to eat them straight away. In the end Jonny let me eat one and we dried out the others.

'I can smell sweets,' said a voice from outside. We recognised the voice straight away.... yes it was Jeremy Mothballs.

'Where's my penny?' I shouted.

'I'll swap it back for a sweet,' he said.

I reluctantly handed him a sweet through the window. He then ran off... without giving me the penny!!!!!

I went red with anger, 'Jonny, we've got to find a way to get our pennies back,' I said.

'Yes, we will,' said Jonny, biting his fingernail.

When the remaining sweets were dried up we ate them and they were absolutely delicious. Jonny had his with a cup of tea and I had mine with a tiny cup of blueberry juice. It was the perfect end to a yumpton (made up word alert) activity.

ACTIVITY NUMBER 13

National Tell a Joke Day

Three days later, Jonny announced that it was national 'tell a joke' day.

'We have to find ten good jokes then tell them to_ each other,' he said.

It was decided that we would put a wooden box in the corner of the room to use as a stage, ready to perform the jokes on later.

I looked in old joke books, comics and on the Internet for ideas. I also remembered a few jokes I'd heard here and there. After seven hours of research I had my ten jokes neatly written on small pieces of cardboard. Jonny had his jokes too, which he hid on a very high up shelf so I wouldn't see them until the performance.

'Let's make popcorn to eat during the show,' I said.

'Eric Trum, that is an excellent idea,' he replied, before rushing into the kitchen. Luckily we had one of those bags of popcorn that go in the microwave and pop away. I waited eagerly, listening to the pops, while feeling slightly nervous about my upcoming

performance.

'Who's going to go first?' asked Jonny as he put the

popcorn into two bowls.

'Me', I said, deciding to get it over and done with,

as I was feeling a little worried about it. I got up onto

the box while Jonny sat on the sofa. I cleared my

throat and looked at my pieces of cardboard. Here are the ten jokes I told.

What dog can jump higher than a building?

- Any dog, buildings can't jump.

How do you know when there's an elephant under your bed?

- When your nose touches the ceiling.

Why didn't the skeleton go to the party?

- Because he had no body to go with.

Why was the boy unhappy to win first prize for the best costume at the Halloween party?

- Because he just came to pick up his sister.

I want a hair cut please.

- Certainly, which one?

What do you call a bear with no teeth?

- A gummy bear.

What is the best way to catch a fish?

- Have someone throw it to you really slowly.

What gets bigger the more you take away?

- A hole in the ground.

What can run all day and never get tired?

- Water.

What is smaller than an ant's dinner?

- An ant's mouth (I know, not very good - but I'd

run out of good jokes and was getting desperate.)

Overall it went quite well, and Jonny actually laughed at numbers one and six. Number ten didn't go quite so well. Jonny just looked at me when I said 'an ant's mouth' and I knew straight away that it was a bad one.

'Doesn't it depend on what the ant had for its dinner?' he asked.

'Well yes, but the ant probably eats something bigger than its mouth on most days,' I said.

'Like what?'

I don't know, what do ants eat?'

Jonny then rushed off to look it up. 'Ok,' he said, coming back downstairs, 'apparently ants will eat almost anything, but they particularly like sweet things.'

'There you go then,' I said, 'so it probably eats something bigger than its mouth.'

'Unless it just eats one grain of sugar,' said Jonny.

'Well it probably eats more than that,' I replied.

'How big is an ant's mouth anyway?' he said.

Oh how I wish I'd picked a better joke for number ten. Oh well, what's done is done.

After one hour on the Internet trying to find out how big an ant's mouth is, Jonny got up and stood on the stage. I sat down and started nibbling on a very large piece of popcorn.

JONNY'S JOKES

Jonny said that he thought it would be hilarious to tell lots of jokes about cheese. I wasn't so sure but nodded politely and waited while he got his notes down from the shelf.

Here is what he came up with.

How do you get a mouse to smile?

*- **Say cheese***

When cheese gets its picture taken what does it say?

 (No answer given)

Knock knock

Who's there?

Cheese

Cheese who?

Cheese a jolly good fellow

What do you call cheese that isn't yours?

*- **Nacho cheese**.*

What type of cheese is made backwards?

- EDAM (quite good).

What do you call a cheese that is big?

- A big cheese. Hmmmmm?

After the sixth joke I slowly tiptoed out of the

room.

Perhaps my ant joke wasn't so bad after all.

Later on we headed out to the shops. We were just

discussing our comedy performances when we saw

Jeremy Mothballs.

'Oh, you're talking about jokes?' he said, walking

over to join us, 'well I've good a good one, what's got

a bottom at the top?'

'I don't know,' said Jonny.

'Legs,' he said laughing, 'and,' he continued,

pointing at me, 'I don't know how your legs manage

to hold your bottom up... it looks so heavy.'

'That's rude,' I said, 'and where's my penny?'

But it was too late... he was gone.

NOTE FROM JONNY

Eric is trying to pretend he didn't like my cheese jokes but he did. In fact, he had to leave the room because he was laughing so much.

ACTIVITY NUMBER 14

Invisible Ink

'A letter has arrived for you,' called Jonny the next morning. I jumped out of bed and raced downstairs. I'd never had a letter before so was more than a little excited.

I leapt up and down, trying to grab the letter out of Jonny's hand.

'Eric, please just wait a minute,' he said. Once I'd stopped jumping he handed me the sealed envelope, which I studied carefully.

It was addressed to Mr Eric Trum, yes that was me.

I checked the address, '41 Brooklands Avenue,' yes,

that was the right address. Then I looked at the

stamp, hmmmmmm, it didn't look quite right. It

seemed to be drawn on in blue biro and had a strange

stick man type queen wearing a wonky crown.

'Are you sure this is a proper stamp?' I asked

Jonny.

He bit his lip, 'Um, I don't know, just open it,' he

said.

I carefully ripped along the top of the envelope

and a piece of cream coloured paper fell out. I picked

it up off the floor; it seemed to be blank.

'Strange,' I said.

'Oh, I know what it'll be,' said Jonny, 'I think

there'll be a message written in invisible ink.'

'Really? So how do I read it?'

'I think you need to heat it up.'

I ran about the house wondering what to do. In the end I held it near a light bulb and sure enough, a message appeared. It said 'WOULD YOU LIKE TO GO ON HOLIDAY WITH ME? FROM JONNY'

It was amazing, the way it appeared.

'I want to reply in invisible ink', I said, 'how do I do it?' I was jumping about all over the place racing around the house and even packing a bag.

METHOD

Put a small amount of lemon juice into an eggcup. (Be very careful not to fall in), Dip a fine paintbrush or cotton bud into the juice and write the message. Let the juice dry.

Hold the paper over a light bulb or put it in the sun and the message should appear.

JONNY'S TOP TIP – *If using a light bulb, ask an adult to help and never use a halogen light bulb, as it could start a fire.*

I wrote my reply and put it in an envelope. I drew my own stamp, wrote 'Jonny' on the front and posted it through the letterbox. Later, Jonny pretended to be extremely surprised to receive a letter. He heated it up and read it. It said....

'I'VE ALREADY PACKED'

HOLIDAY whaaahoooooooo

SCIENCE BIT

Lemon juice is mildly acidic and acid weakens paper. The acid remains in the paper after the juice has dried. When the paper is held near heat, the acidic parts of the paper burn, or turn brown, before the rest of the paper does.

ACTIVITY NUMBER 15

Pebble Doodles

We threw some sleeping bags and food into the back of Jonny's funny orange van.

'Where are you going?' asked Jeremy, coming out of his front door.

'Just on holiday,' said Jonny.

'Won't you be embarrassed to be seen out and about with Eric?' he asked.

Jonny ignored him and continued packing.

I blinked lots of times and hid my bottom amongst the folds of one of the blankets in the back of the van.

Once ready, we got in the front and set off along the country roads. I sat in the middle of the steering wheel, which was great, although I nearly fell off every time we turned a corner.

'Jonny, are you ashamed to be seen with me?' I asked quietly, once we were on a long straight road.

'Of course not, I think you're lovely,' he said.

'Even with this,' I said, pointing at my massive bottom.

'Yes, you are a fantastic stick man, never forget that.'

I smiled and sat, looking straight ahead, feeling on top of the world.

Later on we parked up and went for a walk along the beach. There were lots of pebbles, which made me a little bit sad as I had imagined a beach holiday would involve rolling around on pure white sand.

'Is there a sandy beach here?' I asked.

'No, but Eric, we need a pebbly beach for activity number fifteen.'

We sat down on a blanket and Jonny handed me a felt tip pen. 'Right, I'll give you a pebble and you need to turn it into something by doodling on it with the pen,' he said.

I immediately got to work and changed my pebble into a wonky version of Jeremy Mothballs. I then threw it hard onto the floor.

Jonny made his into a house with two windows and flowers around the door.

We spent six hours on the beach doing the pebble doodle game. I did loads of different doodles, from a poodle, to a pyramid, to a bottom. Quite suddenly it started to get dark so we went back to the van and settled down to sleep in the back.

NOTE – *Use a washable pen so the doodles wash away when the tide comes in.*

ACTIVITY NUMBER 16

Scavenger Hunt

The next day we went back to the beach and sat on the blanket. 'Today, we're going to do a scavenger hunt,' said Jonny. He'd made a long list of items for us to find. 'Right,' he said, handing me my list and a plastic bag, 'you have one hour to find as many of these things as possible.' I studied the list.

A pebble

Seaweed

A stick

Something that you think is beautiful

A piece of litter

A shell

Something red

Something blue

Something smaller than a pea

Something bigger than a football.

'I'm not sure the last one is fair,' I said, 'I'm so small I wont be able to carry something bigger than a football.'

Jonny nodded and crossed it out. 'Right are you ready?'

'Yes,' I said.

'Three, two, one.....go...'

I raced of, dragging my plastic bag behind me.

Jonny rushed off in the other direction with his copy

of the list and his own bag.

One hour later we met back at the blanket. I had managed to find all the items. Jonny had only found two, a pebble and a stick, so I was the winner!!!

YIPEDOOOOODLE.

EXTRA INFORMATION

My red item was a crisp packet.

My Blue item was the sky reflected in a cup of water.

My beautiful item was my smile, (it took quite a lot of persuading before Jonny let me have a point for that one.)

After the scavenger hunt we decided to go home. It had been an excellent holiday but it was great to get back to Brooklands Avenue. I especially appreciated my nice warm bed, as it has been rather cold in the van.

ACTIVITY NUMBER 17

Make a Comic

'Anyone can make a comic,' said Jonny the next week, sitting me down at the table with some pens and five pieces of paper.

'Really, what do I do?' I asked, picking up one of the pens.

METHOD

Planning

Decide who is going to be in your comic, try and have at least two characters then sketch them and write their names underneath.

Next decide on what the comic will be about. Will it have a story, will it just be jokes or will it be completely different to anything anyone has ever done before? If it is going to be a story, make a few notes about what will happen and try and have an idea for an ending (or else the comic might just go on forever and ever.)

I decided to have a two stick men doing stick man jokes.

Do it

After planning out the comic, draw some squares to put the drawings in and, if there is going to be talking, add speech bubbles or bits of writing underneath.

On the next two pages, I'll show you what I came up with.

EXTRA INFORMATION

Jonny did a really weird comic about using PH paper to test if liquids were acids or alkalis. I told him it wasn't a very good topic for a comic, but he said it was going to be brilliant.

1.

2.

3.

PULL YOURSELF TOGETHER

After you've finished, you could photocopy your comic and give it to friends and family. It may even make a brilliant birthday or Christmas present.

My comic took seven days to complete and I was very proud of it. I photocopied my three drawings to give to Jonny. He loved them.

ACTIVITY NUMBER 18

Marble Fun

A few weeks later it was Jonny's birthday and the postman brought him a mysterious parcel.

'What is it?' I said, running around the strangely shaped package, which was wrapped up with brown paper and string.

'Let's see,' he said, carefully undoing the packaging. Inside was a red net bag full of shiny marbles.'

'Wow,' I said, looking at the gleaming glass balls, 'they are amazing, who are they from?'

Jonny looked for a card, but there wasn't one; there was just a piece of paper with a drawing of a spiral on it.

Jonny shrugged and opened the net bag, releasing the marbles, which rolled out onto the floor. 'These are great,' I said, jumping up and trying to balance on one.'

'Hey, let's make playing with marbles be our activity number 18, said Jonny.

'Brilliant,' I said, as I lay down on one and rolled around.

MARBLE GAMES

There are lots of marble games, but we just concentrated on this one...

It's a knock out

For this game we went outside and drew two circles on the ground with chalk. (You can do it inside using string if you prefer). Draw a first circle, which can be any size but we made ours 50 cm in diameter. Then draw another bigger circle around it; our big one was 2 meters in diameter. (The bigger the circles, the harder the game.)

Put four marbles per player in the middle of the inner circle then get ready to play.

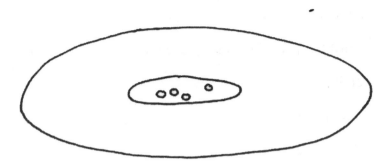

Everyone sits outside the outer circle line and takes it in turns to flick or roll a shooter marble into the middle. The aim is to knock as many marbles as possible out of the inner circle.

If a player manages to knock any out, then they get to collect those marbles and have another go, rolling or flicking from wherever the shooter landed.

If they don't knock any out, then they collect their shooter and it is the next persons go.

The game carries on until all the marbles are collected. The person with the most marbles at the end is the winner.

'Blimey, that's complicated,' I said to Jonny.

'I know,' he said, but let's try it.'

We went outside the front of the house and started drawing the circles on the drive.

'What's going on?' said Jeremy Mothballs through the window.

'Oh nothing much, just um, drawing some circles.'

'I'm good at drawing,' Jeremy said, before coming out with his own piece of chalk. He drew a large bottom inside the inner circle.

'Where's my penny?' I asked.

'I've spent it,' he said.

I looked at him, wondering what to do but ended up just kind of staring with my mouth open, 'I was saving up for a rubber duck,' I said after a while.

'Oh well, never mind,' he replied.

I knew I had to stand up to him, so I took a deep breath, 'you're a mean man Jeremy,' I said, my body shaking slightly. 'You know what I think?' I continued, 'I think you're jealous of all the fun we have.' Jeremy looked at me and then made a sort of growling noise before going back inside.

Jonny and I got on with playing the marble game; I actually did quite well, although I had to roll the marble using both my arms. It was a great struggle and my arms were shaking as I lifted the shooter marble up. However, in the end, I won!! I was mega pleased although my arm muscles were really aching.

After the game we went inside and I lay on the sofa to recover. Jonny put the telly on and played a film about how marbles are made. It was very interesting and showed red-hot flowing glass going into moulds. I watched for a while but I was so tired that I quickly fell asleep.

ACTIVITY NUMBER 19

Live by the Dice!

'Wake up, wake up,' said Jonny. I opened my heavy eyelids and looked at him, I felt like I'd been sleeping for at least a week.

'Oh, is it the morning?' I groaned, sitting upright.

'Yes, you've been asleep for a week and we need to get on with the activities. I've got a great one for today?'

'What is it,' I asked, rubbing my eyes.

'It's called the dice game. All we need is a dice, a pencil and some paper.'

I noticed that he already had a pencil and paper in his hand and there was a shiny red dice next to my knees.

'OK what do we do?' I asked.

'Well, we'll start with breakfast options,' he said, 'we choose six different foods, then roll the dice to choose one at random, and whichever one we get we

HAVE to eat. The only catch is, that one of the options has to be something we wouldn't normally want to eat.'

We began discussing our ideas and came up with this list...

One - *Cornflakes*

Two – *Toast*

Three - *Bread*

Four - *Cheese*

Five - *Cake*

Six - *Chocolate covered ants*

Number six was the one we wouldn't normally have.

I then rolled the dice, and, when it came to a stop we noticed it was a five. Phew, thank goodness it wasn't a six!

We had a wonderful breakfast of cake. Yumalicious.

'Right, let's do it again, lets write a list of six places we could go this morning. We came up with this list as we ate our cake.

One - *The park*

Two - *The library*

Three - *The charity shop*

Four - *Go to the park and spin 100 times on the roundabout (The bad one)*

Five - *Marples coffee shop for more cake*

Six - *Go on a bus*

Jonny rolled this time and got a 6. We ended up getting on the number 88 bus and sat, looking out of the window for about an hour, until we got back to where we'd started.

'This game is quite good,' I said to Jonny, unless you get the bad option.

Once we got home we decided to have another go.

'Let's think of things we could do around the house or garden,' I said.

Here's the list we came up with

One - *Play with the squirt toys in the garden*

Two - *Give Jeremy Mothballs a piece of cake (The bad one)*

Three - *Roll up into a ball and pretend to be a stone*

Four - *Jump 100 times*

Five - *Sit in the garden until wildlife appears*

Six - *Turn a box into a robot*

I stood up, took the dice in two hands then rolled it off the sofa onto the floor. It rolled for ages before eventually coming to a stop. We both watched it, and then my heart stopped. It was a two!!

'Right, you have to take a piece of cake round to Jeremy Mothballs' house,' said Jonny, rushing into the kitchen and reappearing with a nice big piece of gooey chocolate cake on a pink plate.

'I can't,' I stammered, 'I'm kind of scared of him, and he has my penny.'

'You have to, it's the rules of the game,' Jonny said, looking at me with a very serious expression.

I nervously took the cake and walked out of the front door.

'Hello,' I said in a small voice, when Jeremy opened his door.

'What?' he said, looking down at me.

'Would you like a piece of cake? We had some spare,' I held up the cake and he took it before shutting the door. I ran home.

'I did it,' I said, jumping up onto the sofa.

We played the dice game one more time to decided what to watch on TV, then we put the dice away. The game was all a bit too scary for me, although I did enjoy the cake breakfast quite a lot.

ACTIVITY NUMBER 20

Chalk Outlines

Five days later we decided to do activity number twenty. Jonny had got some different coloured chalk sticks form Mr Migow's shop and had placed them neatly on the coffee table.

'I thought we could do body outlines,' he said.

We went outside and I lay on the ground while Jonny drew around me with the chalk. Once I got up again, I was delighted to see my outline on the pavement. I immediately added a smiley face onto the head bit.

Jonny lay down next and I drew around him. It took ages, as he is much bigger than me. Once I'd finished he stood up and I added a funny monster face, 'very funny,' he said, chasing me with the chalk then colouring my face in orange.

We then had a game of guess the object. I had to hide in the loo while Jonny drew around a random object, I then had to come out and guess which object he'd used. It was very obviously a teapot and I got it straight away. I then had a go at drawing round something. Mine was very difficult... it was a pebble. Jonny never got it. Heeeeeheeeeee.

That night we settled down to play Terraria on
Jonny's computer and we talked about what fun we'd
had doing twenty excellent things.

The very next day the most surprising thing of all
happened. As I went outside to see if our chalk
outlines were still there I saw the strangest thing.

'Look at this,' I shouted to Jonny, looking in

amazement at the pavement. He ran out to join me and we stood speechless for a while. There, next to the outline of me, was a new outline. It was a very big outline of a man whose chalk hand was holding my chalk hand! We knew who it was at once.... Yes, it was Jeremy Mothballs. He'd drawn a big smile on his face and, on his top was a strange spiral pattern. As I stared, I noticed something glistening in the middle of the spiral and jumped over to have a look. I couldn't believe it. It was a shiny penny. I picked up the penny immediately and put in my jar.

When I came out again I found Jeremy and Jonny chatting. I went and stood near them, my hands shaking slightly.

'I'm sorry I was mean,' said Jeremy, handing me the pink cake plate. 'I just wanted to play with you, but didn't know how,' he said, looking down.

'Oh,' I mumbled as I struggled to carry it away.

'Let's all be different and life will be brill,' said Jeremy, as I went inside to do the washing up.

After that we got on quite well with Jeremy. He helped us think of games and things to do in the garden. He even lent me his book, '100 Things to do With a Parsnip'.

Well, I'm afraid that's nearly the end of the book. Boo Hoo. But before you go, here is a very special picture of me.

I'm riding my parsnip giraffe!!! Yippee.

I hope you enjoyed reading about our adventures.

Perhaps you might even like to try some of the

activities yourself?

Goodbye for now

From your friend

Eric Trum

Why not try out my activity book?

All you need is a pencil.

13750607R00066

Printed in Great Britain
by Amazon.co.uk, Ltd.,
Marston Gate.